for Maureen and Bernard

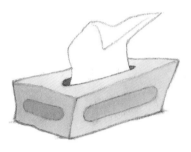

BLOOMSBURY
CHILDREN'S
BOOKS

Published by Bloomsbury, New York and London
Distributed to the trade by Holtzbrinck Publishers.

Library of Congress Cataloging-in-Publication Data available on request

First U.S. Edition 2004
Printed in Hong Kong

1 3 5 7 9 10 8 6 4 2

Bloomsbury USA Children's Books
175 Fifth Avenue
New York, New York 1000

ISBN: 1-58234-926-6

Germs

Ross Collins

BLOOMSBURY
CHILDREN'S
BOOKS

Pox heard Nurse
coming before she arrived.

"Incubating time's up,
Chickenpox 12087-2!" she yelled.
"Time you learned how to be a proper germ!"

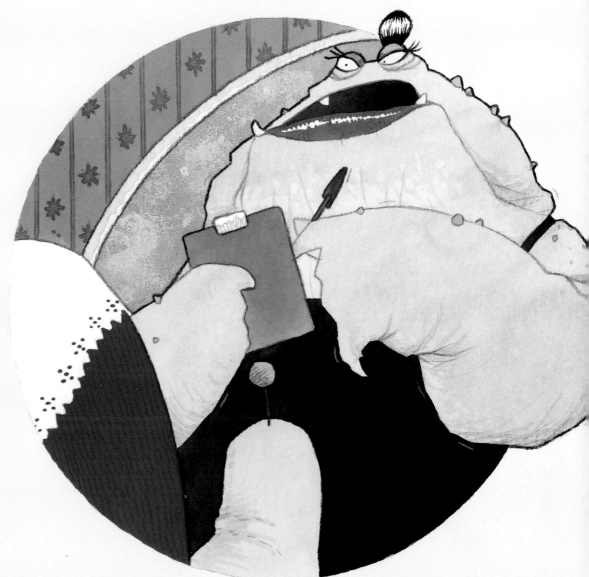

"My friends call me Pox," Pox said, smiling.

"I'm not your friend," snarled Nurse.
"Now pack your bags!"

Later that morning the bubonic bus
arrived to take Pox and the other cadets
to Germ Academy — where minor infections
are turned into real germs.

Once Pox had passed his
physical to prove that he was unhealthy,

he was shown to the dorm
where he met his new roommates.

Rash
MEASLES

Snot
COMMON COLD

After lights out the other germs gathered around Pox to tell stories.
Each boasted of a terrible outbreak which a relative had started.

"But didn't it make the children miserable?" asked Pox.
"That's the point, you numpty," sneered Scab.
But Pox didn't get it.

Medicine Self-Defense

Flight School

All too soon Pox was assigned his first mission.
"But she looks so sweet," said Pox.
"Make her sick," growled Pus.

That night Pox was air dropped outside Myrtle's house and managed to remember enough of his flight training to glide successfully up her left nostril.

Pox slumped against a vein and sulked.
"This job stinks," he thought. "What right have I to..."
But then he heard a noise, getting louder and louder
and heading right for him...

Inside Myrtle, Pox was surrounded.
It was Myrtle's Immune System
and *they* didn't look friendly.

"There he is!" shouted one.
"You picked the wrong kid to infect!" yelled another.

Meanwhile back at Germ Central alarms began to ring.
"The target isn't showing signs of infection!"
barked Commander Phlegm.
"Chickenpox 12087-2 has loused up his mission!"

"Let us go in, sir!"
    sneered Pox's roommates.
"We'll give her a birthday
    she'll never forget, sir!"
"My brave boys," hacked the Commander.

Pox was in trouble.

The Immune System was trained to pulverize
little germs like him.

"Wait!" he shouted, "I'm on your side!"

"Oh yeah – and I'm a fungal infection,"
mocked a voice at the back.

"Why should we trust YOU, germ boy?" scowled another.

"Because four big ugly germs will be coming soon," said Pox,
"and without my help Myrtle could be sick in bed for weeks."

The army paused.

"OK," they said, "What do we do?"

Pox drew up a plan.

Dazed and confused, the germs woke up a minute later.
Rash looked around. "Look," he said, "We made it, we're in!"

They all cheered.
"Let's go infect the little girl!" cried Pus.

They all cheered again.
"What's that noise coming down the tunnel?" asked Scab.

"I don't think we're in Myrtle," gulped Snot.

"Three cheers for Pox!" cried the Immune System.

Pox was hoisted up on shoulders and taken on a triumphant tour of Myrtle. Crowds of cells cheered the germ who had saved them all.

"We've never met a heroic germ before," they said.

"Neither have I," said Pox.

"What can we ever do to repay you?"

"Well," said Pox, "I do need a place to stay..."

Thanks to his germ knowledge Pox was made Honorary Chief of the Immune System. As for Myrtle, haven't you heard?

Well she became...

MIGHTY MYRTLE

MEDICAL M MARVEL

THE GIRL WHO IS NEVER SICK

But that's another story.

FACT FILE

How do germs get in us?
Germs can fly into us from a cough or a sneeze. Or they can be spread by mucky fingers or sharing a sticky sandwich.

How do our bodies fight germs?
Over squillions of years our bodies have worked out how to fight off lots of common germs like Snot and Rash. When they arrive, our Immune System jumps on them until we are well again.

How do we help our bodies to stay healthy?
We can eat good food and exercise to stay healthy. Doctors can help us too with vaccinations and medicines.

Remember, not all germs are nasty. Some of us actually help you lot out — just ask Myrtle.

2/05